WALT DISNEY PRODUCTIONS
presents

Donald Duck:

BOOK CLUB EDITION

Mountain Climber

Random House  New York

Huey, Dewey, and Louie sat in front of
the television set.

They were watching some mountain climbers.

Their uncle, Donald Duck, was reading.

"Uncle Donald!" they shouted.
"Look at these mountain climbers.
They are really good. They could
probably climb the highest mountain
in the world."

"If you think *they* are good," said
Uncle Donald, "you should see *me* climb.
Once upon a time I was the very best
mountain climber anywhere."

Uncle Donald pointed to a photograph on the wall.

"Just look at that picture of me," he said. "Whenever I went mountain climbing, I was always the first to reach the top."

"I didn't know you were a mountain
climber, Uncle Donald," said Huey.

"Why don't you take *us* to some of
those big mountains?" asked Dewey.

"It would be so much fun!" said Louie.

"You know, that sounds like a good idea,"
said Uncle Donald. "I would like to do
some mountain climbing again."

The very next day they packed their bags
and walked down to the train station.

Their friends Mickey and Minnie went
to the station with them, and so did Pluto
and Felix.

"Have a good time!" shouted Mickey.

"And don't forget to be careful," said
Minnie, waving her pink handkerchief.

"Careful?" said Donald. "Don't worry.
You are talking to an expert. I plan to show
these boys a thing or two about climbing
mountains."

All night long the train chugged along,
while Uncle Donald and his nephews slept.
Then, in the early morning, it traveled
through a long, dark mountain tunnel.
When the train came out of the tunnel—
into the bright sunshine—the boys woke up.

"Wow! Look at those mountains!"
shouted Louie.

"Did *you* ever climb mountains like those?"
Dewey asked his uncle.

Donald looked out the window at the white,
snowy peaks.

"Of course I climbed mountains like those,"
he said. "And even higher!"

At last the train stopped at an old-fashioned mountain village.

Carrying their bags, Uncle Donald and his three nephews walked down the main street.

They stopped in front of the village inn.

"I'm Donald Duck, the mountain climber,"
said Uncle Donald. "Do you have a room
for me and my three nephews?"

"Indeed I do," said the innkeeper, shaking
Donald's hand. "Let me show it to you."

Huey, Dewey, and Louie were very excited.
They wanted to go climbing right away.
"When can we get started, Uncle Donald?"
they asked.

"Now just a minute!" said Uncle Donald.
"Mountain climbing is very hard. You will
have time enough for that when you are older.
The three of you can have a good time here
at the inn while *I* am climbing."

Leaving his unhappy nephews at the inn,
Donald went out to look for a store.

He stopped in front of
a shop window filled with
things for mountain climbing.

"Wow!" he said. "This is
the place for me. I see
everything I need."

Goofy's
Ski Shop

"Good morning, Mr. Shopkeeper," said Donald.
"I am Donald Duck, the mountain climber."

"You have come to just the right place,
Mr. Duck," said the shopkeeper. "I have
everything you need—even a good guide.
Goofy's my name, and I'm the best guide
in the whole village."

"First, you must have some good strong rope
and some metal spikes," said Goofy. "Then you
will want a hammer and a climbing ladder."

"And of course you have to have a back pack
and some skis," Goofy added, putting on his hat.
"Now . . . just follow your trusty guide."
Poor Donald could hardly walk under the load!

Huey, Dewey, and Louie came out
to say good-by.

"Please, Uncle Donald," they begged.
"Won't you let us go, too?"

"Sorry, boys," said Donald.
"This mountain climbing is only
for experts like me. You stay here."

Looking very sad, Huey, Dewey,
and Louie waved good-by.

"This is certainly the life!" said Guide Goofy
with a big grin.

He walked briskly up the trail.

Poor Donald followed, huffing
and puffing under his load.

"Somebody must have slipped
a ton of lead into this pack,"
he grumbled.

Up, up, up
they climbed.

Goofy went so fast that
he pulled Donald right along
behind him.

Finally Goofy came to a steep
cliff. He had to hammer steel spikes
into the rock for a foothold.

Rock chips began
to fall on Donald
down below.

"Hey! Watch what you're
doing!" shouted Donald.

He lost his hold
on the rock and went
spinning out into
space. Sharp rocks
spattered all around him.

"You call yourself
a guide?"

Donald shook
his hammer
at Goofy.

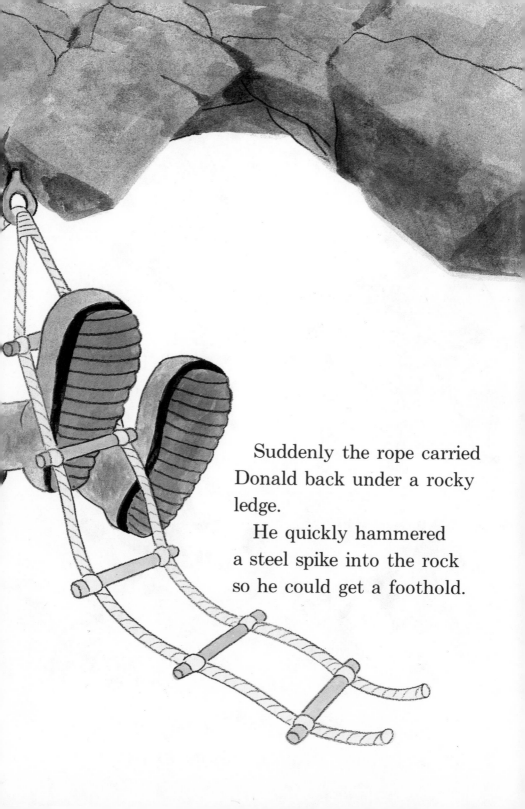

Suddenly the rope carried
Donald back under a rocky
ledge.

He quickly hammered
a steel spike into the rock
so he could get a foothold.

Just as Donald pulled himself up over the rocky ledge, snow began to fall.

"What do you know?" said Goofy. "It's snowing!"
"Yes, I know," snapped Donald. "I can see it."

Donald strapped on his skis and started up the slope behind Goofy.

They had not gone far when Goofy's climbing stick hit a huge ball of snow.

Down rolled the snowball, knocking Donald flat on his back and covering him with snow.

Back at the inn, Huey, Dewey, and Louie
went ice-skating.

Then they
rode downhill
on a long sled.
But after a while
they became restless.

They decided to look around the village.

At the town square they
saw a big sign that said:

**CABLE CAR
TO THE
MOUNTAINTOP**

Digging down into their
pockets, Huey, Dewey, and
Louie found just enough money
to buy tickets for the cable car.

TICKETS

Soon they were sailing high above the village.

As they waved to the people down below, Huey said, "This is the life!"

"It certainly beats climbing," Dewey agreed.

Swaying back and forth,
the little car climbed steadily
toward the faraway mountain peak.
The boys felt as if they were
flying.

Far below they could see two tiny figures struggling up the mountain.

But they did not recognize their Uncle Donald and his guide, Goofy.

"Look at those silly billies," said Huey. "They must have started a long time ago."

"I bet we'll beat them to the top," said Huey.

When the cable car slid into the station
at the mountain peak, the nephews
raced out of the car
and up the stairs to
the lookout point.

WORLD'S BEST VIEW!

Huey grabbed the long, black telescope and pointed it at the two tiny figures on the slope down below.

One of the tiny figures
was Uncle Donald, covered
with a snowball and a very
surprised mountain goat.

The other figure was Guide Goofy
stuck in a snowbank up to his waist.

The three boys rushed off to the supply hut
as fast as they could go.

Back they came with a long, stout rope.
Huey tied one end of the rope around
the railing on the lookout tower.
Down, down, down it fell—coil after coil—
until it reached the climbers far below.

Tugging with all their might, Huey, Dewey, and
Louie managed to pull the two frozen mountain
climbers up to
the top of the
lookout tower.

Goofy looked around
in amazement.
"Gosh!" he said.
"This is really a great view
I never climbed to the top
of a mountain before."

When Uncle Donald heard Goofy say that,
he was too angry to speak.

Squawking with rage, he threw his climbing
equipment in all directions.

THIS WAY
DOWN!

Then, with a great shove,
he pushed Goofy off the peak—
into a snowbank far below.

"Now that you've seen
the peak," he shouted, "take
a good look at the bottom."

"Come on, boys,"
said Donald. "We
are taking the cable
car down!"

"This is really fun," Donald's nephews shouted as the cable car swayed back and forth.

"Look at the view, Uncle Donald. Doesn't this feel just like a flying ship?"

Poor Uncle Donald was feeling too sick to answer

"We love the mountains," said Huey.
"Can we come up here again tomorrow?"
Uncle Donald shook his arms with rage.
The great mountain climber never
wanted to see another mountain as long
as he lived!